By Air, Sea, an
Cars

Paul Stickland

WATERBIRD BOOKS
Columbus, Ohio

Hatchback Car

Although it is a small car, **hatchbacks** can hold a lot of groceries.

Sport Utility Vehicle

A **sport utility vehicle**, or SUV, is built to go almost anywhere.

More About Hatchback Cars

Hatchbacks are easy to drive because they are so small. Because hatchbacks are small and light, they need only small engines.

More About Sport Utility Vehicles

Most SUVs have four-wheel drive. Each wheel gets power from the engine. Big tires help SUVs travel safely across mud, rocks, and snow.

Station Wagon

A **station wagon** has a lot of room for family, friends, and pets.

More About Station Wagons

Station wagons can transport many people at one time.
The luggage rack on top of the station wagon is used to
carry large items like luggage.

There are three rows of seats in this station wagon.
The rear seats can be folded down flat to fit more items.

Convertible Car

Convertible cars have tops that fold down.

Some people still drive **old-fashioned cars**.

More About Convertible Cars

This car has a soft top that is made out of waterproof fabric. It has to be put down by hand. Other convertibles have tops made out of metal.

More About Old-Fashioned Cars

Old-fashioned cars did not provide much protection from the weather. The roof was made of canvas and would let the rain leak through.

Monster Truck

Monster trucks have large tires that are bigger than some other cars.

It looks huge next to a little car.

More About Monster Trucks

Monster trucks should not drive on the road.
They are too big for the roads and may not fit
under bridges.

Monster trucks are built using parts from other kinds of
vehicles. The huge tires come from a tractor.

Motor Home

Motor homes provide room for a family to live while traveling.

More About Motor Homes

This motor home is like a small house. It has a kitchen, bathroom, and bed. Motor homes also have electricity and running water, making it easier to travel.

When traveling for long distances, people can sleep and eat in the motor home, as well as travel. At night, the motor home can stop at a campsite and spend the night before moving on the next day.

What Did You Learn?

How are these two vehicles different?

How would you get all of these cars down?

Why is this car so long? What is it used for?

What is this car built for?   Where is the top of this car?

This streamlined car is built for speed. Being low off the ground helps the car make sharp turns.

This stretch limousine is used by groups of people traveling in style together. There is a lot of room inside, and the seating is luxurious.

This car is high enough to clear rocks when it is driving over rough ground.

This car has airfoils that help to keep it stable while it is going very fast. Airfoils are similar to airplane wings.

Using the controls in the cab, the driver will lower the tailgate. The driver will reverse all cars out from the lower level of the supporter, then lower the top level to the ground and reverse out.

This car is a convertible. Its top has been folded back.

School Specialty
Children's Publishing

Copyright © Paul Stickland 1992, 2004
Designed by Douglas Martin.

This edition published in the United States of America in 2004 by
Waterbird Books,
an imprint of School Specialty Children's Publishing,
a member of the School Specialty Family.
8720 Orion Place, Columbus, OH 43240-2111
www.ChildrensSpecialty.com

Library of Congress Cataloging-in-Publication is on file with the publisher.

ISBN 0-7696-3373-0
Printed in China.
1 2 3 4 5 6 7 8 MP 08 07 06 05 04